LADYBIRD  CLASSICS

GULLIVER'S
Travels

by Jonathan Swift

Retold by Marie Stuart
Illustrated by Ciaran Duffy

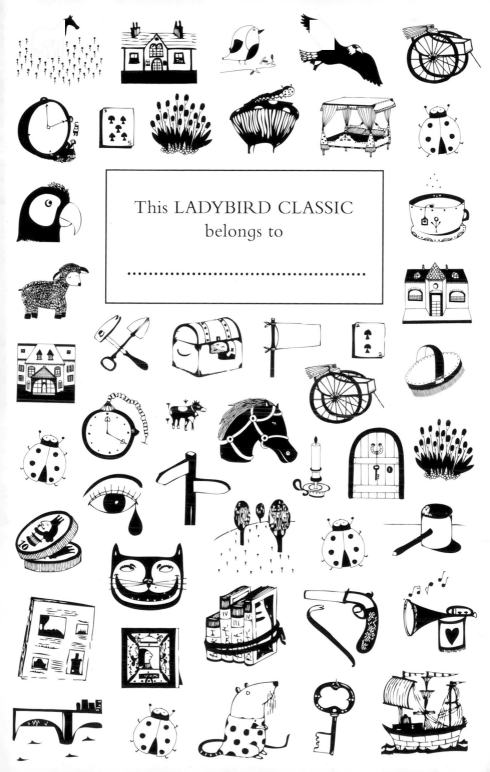

This LADYBIRD CLASSIC
belongs to

....

A History of the Author

Jonathan Swift was born in Dublin in 1667. He did many things in his life – he was secretary to the author and diplomat Sir William Temple, he became an Anglican priest and was made Dean of St Patrick's Cathedral in Dublin, and he was involved in politics – but he is best known for his satirical writing, especially *Gulliver's Travels*.

Chapter illustrations by Valeria Valenza

A catalogue record for this book is available from the British Library

Published by Ladybird Books Ltd
80 Strand London WC2R 0RL
A Penguin Company

001 – 10 9 8 7 6 5 4 3 2 1

ISBN: 978-1-40931-127-0

Printed in China

Contents

Chapter One

My Arrival in a Strange Land

I WAS FOR some years a physician in London, but my business had begun to fail. So, having consulted with my wife, I decided to go to sea. On May 4th, 1699, I said goodbye to my family and set sail from Bristol as a ship's doctor bound for the South Seas.

All went well for the first few weeks. Then there was a bad storm and the ship was wrecked. Six of the crew, of whom I was one, got into a little boat and began to row to an island nearby. Suddenly a huge wave upset the boat, and all the other men were lost. Only I, Lemuel Gulliver, was left.

I swam as long as I could and at last, just as I could swim no more, my feet touched the bottom. I waded through the water to the shore, where there was no sign of houses or people.

I walked about half a mile further, but still saw no one. Tired out, I lay down on the short, soft grass and went to sleep.

When I woke up it was daylight. I lay still for a moment, wondering where I was, then tried to get up. I could not move my arms or my legs or my head! I was tied to the ground! There was a buzzing noise near me, but I could not see what was making it.

Suddenly I felt something moving on

my left leg. It walked up me and stopped close by my chin. I looked down as well as I could (for my hair was tied to the ground) and saw a tiny man, less than six inches high, with a bow and arrow in his hand. Then many more of these little men started to run all over me. I was so surprised that I roared loudly. They ran back in fright and fell over one another trying to get away. I found out later that some of them had hurt themselves when they fell from my chest.

I managed to break the strings that tied my left arm to the ground, and pulled some of my hair loose so that I could move my head. This made the little men even more afraid, and they shot arrows at me. Some fell on my hands and some on my face, pricking me like needles and making my skin sore wherever they landed.

The little men stood around at a

distance, watching me. After a while, when they saw that I was not going to hurt them, they cut some of the strings that bound me. This at least allowed me to move my head more freely.

Now I could see that they had built a little platform beside my head so that they could talk to me. A well-dressed gentleman climbed up and began to speak to me. He spoke for some time, but I could not understand him, and I began to grow hungry. I pointed to my mouth and pretended to chew. He seemed to understand and at once sent men to bring me food and drink.

Ladders were put against my sides, and over a hundred of the little men climbed up, bringing baskets of meat and bread. Each piece of meat was the size of one small piece of mince, so I had to keep asking for more. The loaves were so tiny that I ate three at a time.

I drank a whole barrel of their wine at a gulp, which was not difficult to do, as the barrel held hardly half a pint. They kept looking at each other as if they could not believe it was possible to drink so much, but they brought me some more wine, which I drank as well.

I made signs to let them know I would not try to escape, and they loosened the strings so that I could turn on my side. They also put some ointment on my face and hands, which took away the soreness their arrows had caused.

Then I fell asleep again.

CHAPTER TWO

The Emperor

WHEN I WOKE up I found myself on
a kind of platform with wheels. It was
moving towards the capital city of these
tiny people, about half a mile away.
Fifteen hundred large horses, each about
as big as my hand, were pulling me along.
I later found out that it had taken five
hundred carpenters and engineers to
make this platform, and no less than nine

hundred men to put me onto it while I was still asleep.

For some time I did not know what had wakened me. I was told later, however, that some of the young people wanted to see how I looked when I was asleep. They climbed onto the platform and walked very softly up to my face. One of them, an officer in the Guards, put the sharp end of his spear up into my nose, which tickled my nose like a straw and made me sneeze, waking me up. They ran away quickly, before I caught sight of them.

We made a long march for the remainder of that day and rested at night. They put five hundred guards on each side of me, ready to shoot me if I tried to escape.

At last we arrived at the capital. The platform to which I was tied stopped outside a temple that was no longer used. Since this was the largest building in the

whole country, the emperor had planned that I should live there. The door was just big enough for me to creep through when I wanted to sleep. Once inside, I could only lie down.

The little men, however, would not let me go free. They put nearly a hundred of their tiny chains around my left leg so that, although I could stand up, I could not move very far.

When this was done, the emperor visited me. He carried in his hand a sword about as big as one of our darning needles, to defend himself if I should break loose. He was a handsome little man, much taller than the rest of his court, and he wore a gold helmet with a plume on the crest. All the ladies and gentlemen of the court, who were with him, were dressed in gold and silver, which flashed in the sun.

I tried to answer the emperor when he

spoke to me, but he could not understand any of the many languages I speak. Soon he went away to decide whether he would have to have me killed or not, for I would cost a great deal to feed, and might be dangerous.

After the emperor had gone away, a great crowd of the tiny people came to see me because none of them had ever seen such a big person before. Some of the men shot arrows at me, and one just missed my eye. The guards tied these men up and gave them to me to punish.

I put five of them in my pocket and pretended I was going to eat the other one, who was very frightened. Then I took out my penknife and cut the cords that bound him, and set him on the ground. I treated the other five in the same way, taking them out of my pocket one by one; everyone was very surprised to see me treat them so gently.

Two of the guards went to the emperor to tell him what I had done. He decided that since I had been kind to his people, he would not have me killed. He ordered people who lived close to the town to bring me six cows and forty sheep every day, and wine to drink. This was only just enough for me, since everything was so tiny.

Three hundred tailors were told to make clothes for me, and six hundred of the little people were to look after me. They were to live in tents outside the temple to make it easier for them. Lastly, six men were to teach me their language.

CHAPTER THREE

I Am Searched

THREE WEEKS LATER, I was able to understand and talk to the little men. The first thing I asked the emperor for was freedom. He said that they must first see if I was carrying anything that could be a danger to his people. Two men came to look through my pockets, and wrote down everything they found. They gave me a new name – the Great Man Mountain.

In my pockets they found:

A handkerchief, which they thought was like a carpet.

A snuffbox, which they called a chest filled with dust. It made them sneeze.

A notebook, in which they recognized very large handwriting.

A comb. They knew what this was for, but said it looked like the railings around the emperor's palace.

A knife, a razor and a pair of pistols. All these things were new to them, and they could not think what they were for.

A watch. They said it made a noise like a water mill. They thought it must be a god that I worshipped, because I told them I always looked at it before I did anything.

A purse. They called this a net large enough for a fisherman, but they knew I used it as a purse. They were very surprised at the size of the gold pieces in my purse.

When the two little men had finished

looking in my pockets, they looked at my belt. They wrote down that I had a sword as long as five men and a pouch with two pockets. One of these pockets held black powder, the other very heavy round balls.

They took their list to the emperor, who asked me to take out my sword and put it carefully on the ground. Then he asked me what my pistols were for. I told him not to be afraid, and I fired one of them in the air.

Everyone fell down in fright except the emperor, although he, too, went very white. He made me give up my pistols at once. I did so, telling him that the black powder must be kept away from fire because it was very dangerous.

All my things were put away in the emperor's storeroom, except for my eyeglasses, which were in a pocket the men had not found.

Slowly the emperor and his people

came to understand that they were in no danger from me. From time to time some of them would dance on my hand, and the boys and girls liked to play hide-and-seek in my hair as I lay on the ground. Even the horses stopped being afraid of me, and horses and riders would take turns to leap over my hand as I held it on the ground.

CHAPTER FOUR

I Am Set Free

ONE DAY SOME people came to tell
the emperor that they had found a huge,
black object lying on the ground, and they
thought it might belong to the Great Man
Mountain. It was my hat, which I thought
I had lost at sea! To bring it to me, they
made two holes in the brim and fastened
cords from the hat to the harnesses of
five horses. It was then dragged along the

ground for half a mile. This did not do it much good!

Another time the emperor asked me to stand with my legs apart so that his army could march between them. There were no less than three thousand foot soldiers and one thousand horsemen, and they marched with drums beating and flags flying.

I asked once more to be set free, and at last the emperor agreed, as long as I would obey his rules. I said that I would, and my chains were taken off.

I had always wanted to see the capital city, and now that I was free the emperor said I could. All the people were told to stay in their houses in case I walked on them. So they crowded to their little windows to see me as I stepped over the wall into the city where the emperor's palace stood.

It was really magnificent, like a big

doll's house. I lay down to look inside and the empress came to the window, smiling, and gave me her hand to kiss.

Soon after I was set free, one of the country's great men came to see me. We had a long talk, and I learned many things.

I had thought the island, which was called Lilliput, was a peaceful and happy one, but he told me this was not so.

'You may have seen,' he said, 'that some of us wear high heels and some wear low heels on our shoes. The emperor will let only people wearing low heels work for him, and those who like high heels feel that this is wrong. Because of this there are many quarrels among the Lilliputians.'

Then he told me of a much bigger danger that was about to befall his country.

'There is an island close by called Blefuscu, and the people there are going to attack us.'

'Why?' I asked him.

'It all began a long time ago,' he replied. 'When our emperor's great-grandfather was a little boy, he cut his finger one morning as he took the top off his egg. Up till then everyone had cut off the big end of the egg. After that, however, the ruler of those times said that everyone must cut off the small end, and those who would not obey had to leave Lilliput. They went to the island of Blefuscu and called themselves the Big-Endians. Now they are coming to make war on Lilliput, and the emperor wants you to help us.'

CHAPTER FIVE

Peace is Restored

I SAID I would help the people of Lilliput
in any way I could, for they had been
very kind to me.

I knew that the Big-Endians had about
fifty war ships lying at anchor, and I
planned to seize them.

I fixed fifty hooks to fifty lengths of
cord, then set off for Blefuscu. There was
only about half a mile of sea between the

islands, and I could wade most of the way.

The enemy took fright when they saw me, and leapt out of their ships and swam to shore. I then fastened a hook to the prow of each ship, and tied all the cords together at the end. While I was doing this, the Big-Endians shot thousands of their tiny arrows at me. I was afraid one would go in my eye, so I put on my glasses.

After I had cut the anchor cables, I took up the knotted end of the cords to which my hooks were tied, and set off back to Lilliput with fifty of the enemy's largest ships.

The emperor was so pleased with me that he made me a nardac, which is something like a duke in my own land. He now wanted me to seize the rest of the enemy's ships, so that he could be emperor of the Big-Endians as well as Lilliput. He would then be able to make

the Big-Endians obey his rules and cut off
the small ends of their eggs. I would not
do this, as I did not think it was right. This
made the emperor angry with me.

Soon after this, some of the Big-
Endians came to make peace with the
Lilliputians. When they saw me again,
they asked me to come to Blefuscu one
day so that everyone could see how big
I was. I said that I would, which made
the emperor even more angry with me.
His chief admiral was displeased with me,
too, not only because it was I who had
defeated the Big-Endian navy (which he
could not do), but also because I had been
made a nardac.

There were others amongst the
emperor's great men who did not like me,
some of them because I ate so much of
their food, and some who thought I was
dangerous. They all asked the emperor
to have me put to death as an enemy of

Lilliput, because I had refused to do what the emperor wanted.

The emperor refused to have me put to death, because I had helped him. He thought for a long time, then said that the best way to punish me would be to put out my eyes.

One of the great men was my friend. He came in secret to tell me what the emperor had said, so that I could save myself.

When I heard what he had to say, I felt that the time had come for me to leave Lilliput, and save myself from being blinded.

CHAPTER SIX

I Return Home

I WENT DOWN to the shore and took
one of the emperor's ships. I put my clothes
in it so that they would not get wet, and
pulled it after me as I swam across to
Blefuscu.

The emperor of Blefuscu was pleased
to see me, and so were all his people. They
were kind to me, and I liked them, but I did
not want to spend the rest of my life there.

One day I saw, out at sea, a full-sized boat floating upside down. I asked the emperor for some ships and men to help me bring it to shore, so that I could sail home in it.

It took two thousand of the tiny men to help me turn the boat the right way up once it was ashore. Then I had to get ready for the long journey home.

The thickest linen these people had was much thinner than that of our finest handkerchiefs, so thirteen thicknesses were put together to make two sails for me. It took five hundred workmen to make them!

I made ropes and cables by twisting together as many as thirty of the thickest and strongest of their ropes. I made oars and masts with the help of the emperor's ship carpenters. A large, heavy stone that I found by the seashore would serve as an anchor.

When all was ready, I stored food on-board, and also live cows and bulls and sheep, which I wanted to show my family. I would have liked to take some of the little people with me, but the emperor would not allow me to.

It took about a month to complete the preparations. When all was ready I set off, and two days later I saw a big ship, whose captain took me on-board. He did not believe my story until he saw the live cows and sheep, which were in my pocket.

When at last I got home, my wife and children were very happy to see me again and to hear all my adventures. As for the cows and sheep, I put them to eat grass in a park close by my house, at Greenwich in London. There they thrived, and they have since increased greatly in number!

CHAPTER SEVEN

Another Adventure

I STAYED AT home with my family for just two months. Then the yearning for travel overtook me again, and I set sail once more aboard a merchant ship called the *Adventure*.

The first part of our voyage was pleasant, with nothing to trouble us. But one day a bad storm blew up, and we were driven hundreds of miles out of our way.

We were lost. There was plenty of food on-board, but not nearly enough water. So when the lookout in the topmast spotted land, the captain sent several of us ashore to get water.

When we landed, there was no sign of a river or spring, nor of any inhabitants. The other men kept to the shore, while I walked inland. The country seemed barren and rocky, with no water to be seen, and so I turned back.

From where I stood, I could see our ship's boat with all the men on-board, rowing as quickly as they could back to the ship. They had left me behind! Then I saw why. There was a huge man-like creature chasing them, taking great strides through the sea.

I did not wait to see what might happen. I ran away as fast as I could and climbed a steep hill. From there I could see what the surrounding country was like.

I could not believe my eyes! The grass was nearly as tall as a house, with corn towering above it as high as a church steeple!

I walked along what I thought was a main road, but which I found out later was just a footpath to the people of this land. At last I came to a stile.

Each step in this stile was like a high wall to me, and I could not climb it. As I was looking for a gap in the huge hedge, I saw another enormous man like the one I had seen chasing my friends. I was very frightened, and ran to hide in the corn.

He called out in a voice that sounded to me like thunder, and seven other giants like himself came towards him. They carried scythes, each as big as six of our own, to reap the corn.

I grew even more frightened. Where could I hide? I ran to and fro to keep out of their way, but they moved too fast for me to escape.

At last, just as one was about to step on me, I called out 'Stop!' as loudly as I could. The man looked down and picked me up, holding me tightly in case I should bite him. I tried to let him know, by groaning and turning my head from side to side, how much he was hurting me. He seemed to understand, and eased his grip. Then he took me to his master to show him what he had found. This man was a farmer, and the same man I had seen at first in the field.

The farmer pulled out his handkerchief, wrapped me in it, and took me back to his farm. His wife screamed and ran away when she saw me, just as my wife does when she sees a mouse!

Then the three children came to have a look at me. They were just going to have their dinner, and they put me on the table, where they could see me as they ate.

It was like being on the roof of a house. I was in a terrible fright, and kept as far as I could from the edge, for fear of falling.

The farmer's wife gave me some crumbs of bread and minced up some meat for me. I took out my knife and fork and started to eat, which delighted them. The farmer's wife filled her smaller cup (it was as big as a bucket) with cider for me, but I could not drink it all!

Then in came the nurse with the baby in her arms. He wanted me as a plaything. When they gave me to him, he put my head in his mouth. I roared so loudly that the baby was frightened and dropped me. I would have been killed if his mother had not caught me in her apron.

After dinner the farmer went back to his fields, and his wife put me to bed with a handkerchief over me for a sheet. The bed was as wide as a main road in England, and the handkerchief thicker

than the mainsail of a ship!

Later on, the daughter of the house made a bed for me in the baby's cradle. This girl was very good to me. She was nine years old and small for her age in that country, since she was only forty feet tall! She called me Grildrig, which meant 'Little Man', and taught me to speak their language. I liked her very much.

CHAPTER EIGHT

Life Among the Giants

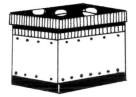

AS SOON AS the people who lived round about heard of me, they all came to have a look at me. One of them told the farmer that he should take me to town next market day and make people pay to see me.

So the farmer put me into a little box that had some holes in it to allow me to breathe, and on the next market day he set off with me. His little girl came with us to look after me. She was very worried in case some harm should come to me, and she put a little quilt in the box to make me more comfortable. I was grateful for her company, and I called her my nurse.

As soon as we arrived in town, the farmer took me to an inn he frequented. There I was placed on a table, and people were invited in to see me. I did all the funny tricks I could think of: I stood on my head, I hopped about and I danced. I picked up a thimble, which my nurse had given me for a cup, and I drank everyone's health.

The spectators were delighted, and the room filled nearly to bursting with all those who wanted to watch me.

The farmer made a great deal of money from showing me on market day, and he decided to take me to other towns. So we travelled round the country, and I

was shown in many towns, villages and private homes. At last, after several weeks, we came to the capital city, where the royal family lived.

The queen liked me so much that she bought me from the farmer. I begged her to let my nurse stay with me, and she agreed. The farmer gave his consent as well, and the little girl could barely hide her joy.

The queen had a little room made for me, with a roof that lifted up and furniture that was just the right size for me. To them it was a small box, which could be attached to a belt for carrying. The queen had a set of silver cups, saucers and plates made for me, too. It was like a doll's tea set to her!

I always had my meals at a little table on the queen's table, just at her left elbow. It upset me to see the way the queen ate. She would put a piece of bread as big as

two of our loaves in her mouth at one go!
Her dinner knife was taller than me, and I
thought it looked very dangerous.

Every Wednesday, which was their
Sunday, the king came to have dinner
with us. He liked to talk and ask
questions about England. He wanted to
know in what ways we were different
from the people in his own country of
Brobdingnag.

The only member of court I did not
get along with was the queen's dwarf. He
was five times as tall as me – about thirty
feet – but this was small to his people. The
king was twice as tall as he was! He was
jealous because the queen seemed to like
me better than him, and he played tricks
on me. Once he dropped me in a jug of
cream. I swam to the side and my nurse
fished me out. The queen became so
cross with the dwarf that she finally sent
him away.

I was pleased when they made a little boat for me and put it in a tub of water so that I could row about. Sometimes they put a sail on the boat. Then the queen and her women would make a breeze for me with their fans. They liked to see how well I could steer. It was great fun for me.

Sometimes, however, life in Brobdingnag was no fun at all! Once, when I was sitting at my table eating breakfast, about twenty wasps swarmed in through an open window. They were as big as our pigeons, and their buzzing sounded like the drones of an army of bagpipes. Worst of all, their stings were as long as my thumb and sharp as needles! As they flew about my head and face, I managed to fight them off with my dagger.

On another day, a monkey came into my room and picked me up. I think he took me for a baby monkey, for he

stroked my face gently as he held me.

Suddenly there was a noise at the door, and he leapt through the window and up to the roof, carrying me with him. The servants had to get ladders and climb up in order to drive the monkey away and bring me down.

CHAPTER NINE

An Eventful Journey

ONE DAY WHEN the king and I were talking, I said I could teach him to make gunpowder so that he could win a lot of wars. The king, however, was horrified when I explained to him how gunpowder works, and described the destruction that guns can cause. He said that he would rather lose half his kingdom than use such weapons, and told me I must never speak of them again. If a man could make two ears of corn, or two blades of grass grow where only one grew before, said the king, he would do more good than he could ever do by winning a war.

Soon after this the king and queen and their servants set off on a long journey to another part of Brobdingnag. I went with them in my box. They fixed up a hammock in it so that I should not feel the bumps so much as we went along.

My nurse came too, but she got a bad cold on the way. When at last we came to a stop, she had to rest in bed for a few days.

I knew we were near the sea, and I longed to see it again. Since my nurse was confined to her bed, one of the queen's pages was told to take me down to the seashore.

My nurse did not want to let me go, almost as if she had some foreboding of what was to happen. But at last, in floods of tears and with many warnings to the page to be careful, she consented.

I was put into my box, and the boy carried me to the rocky coast, where I asked to be set down. I lay in my hammock, looking out at the sea and feeling sad. When would I see my home again?

After some time the page went off to look for birds' eggs, and I fell asleep.

I awoke suddenly with a jolt. There was a loud swishing noise above me, and my box seemed to be moving upwards very fast. I called out several times, but no one answered.

Then I guessed what had happened. A big bird, perhaps an eagle, had swooped down and picked up my box in his beak. I was flying through the air!

Soon there came a loud squawking, as if the eagle were fighting, and all at once

I was falling. Faster and faster, down, down, down! My box stopped with a great splash!

CHAPTER TEN

The Voyage Home

AFTER A MOMENT I stopped trembling and looked out of the window. I was at sea!

I pulled open a little trap door in the roof of my box to let in some fresh air. Then I called for help, but no one heard me. How I wished my nurse was with me!

I took out my handkerchief and tied it to my walking stick. Then I stood on a chair and pushed this flag through the little trap door, waving it to and fro and calling for help again. No one came, and I gave myself up for lost.

I sat without hope for a long time. Then, as I stared through the window, I suddenly realized that my box was being pulled along.

After a little while it stopped, and there was a clattering above my head like that of a cable being passed through the ring on top. Once more I pushed my flag out of the trap door and called for help.

This time, to my great joy, someone answered – in English! I begged him to come and let me out. He told me that I was safe, and that my box was tied to the side of his ship. He said he would send someone to cut a hole in it.

Soon this was done, and with the help of a ladder and many willing hands, I was pulled up onto the deck.

It was an English ship, with English sailors – not giants, not little men, but people the same size as me!

The sailors asked me why I had been in the box. When I told them my story, they did not believe me. At first the captain thought I had been shut up in the box because I had done something very bad.

When I told him about the country and people of Brobdingnag, he did not believe me either. I was not surprised, so I showed him a gold ring the queen had given me – it was so big I wore it round my neck like a collar. And I gave him a giant's tooth which a Brobdingnagian dentist had taken out by mistake. It was as big as a wine bottle!

At last the men believed me. The captain said he would take me back to England with him, and we set sail for home.

Many weeks later, when I left the ship

and came on land again, the houses and people all looked so small compared to those of Brobdingnag that, for a moment, I thought I must be in Lilliput once more. And when my wife heard about the dangers I had been through, she said I must never go to sea again.

For myself, I was glad to be back with my family and home – I had had enough adventure for quite some time!

Collect more fantastic

LADYBIRD  CLASSICS

9781409311232

9781409311256

9781409311287

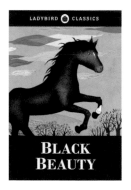

9781409311249

9781409311270

9781409311263